BEGINNER READER

RAINBOW magic™

Pet Parade

Orchard Beginner Readers are specially created to develop literacy skills, confidence and a love of reading.

ORCHARD BOOKS
First published in the USA in 2013 by Scholastic Inc
First published in Great Britain in 2017 by The Watts Publishing Group
This edition published in 2018 by The Watts Publishing Group

3 5 7 9 10 8 6 4 2

A CIP catalogue record for this book is available from the British Library.

ISBN 978 1 40834 579 5

Printed in China

The paper and board used in this book are made from wood from responsible sources
Orchard Books
An imprint of Hachette Children's Group
Part of The Watts Publishing Group Limited
Carmelite House, 50 Victoria Embankment, London EC4Y 0DZ

An Hachette UK Company
www.hachette.co.uk
www.hachettechildrens.co.uk

RAINBOW magic™

Pet Parade

Daisy Meadows

ORCHARD

The Pet Fairies are enjoying a sunny day with their pets.

A pretty tune floats through the forest, and a tiny blue bird flies into the clearing. It's Flit!

Flit is a royal messenger.
He drops a red envelope into Bella's hands.
She opens it and reads the note.

"The king and queen need our help," Bella announces. "They want an animal friend of their very own!"

What is the best pet for the fairy king
and queen?
"They must get a loyal goldfish," Molly says.
"No, a cuddly hamster," Harriet insists.
The Pet Fairies cannot agree.

"Let's take lots of pets to the palace," Georgia suggests. "Then the king and queen can pick the perfect one."

"It will be a pet parade!" Katie exclaims.

The first stop is a farmyard.
Two ponies join Penny's in a grassy green field.

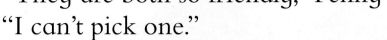

"They are both so friendly," Penny says.
"I can't pick one."
Penny takes both ponies.

Katie opens the tall, red barn doors.
Some kittens are playing in the hay.
"They are too cute!" says Katie. "I
can't pick just one."
She lifts four kittens in her arms and
puts them in the cart.

Behind the barn, Harriet finds some hamsters.
"They are all so furry," Harriet says.
She gently places three hamsters in a crate.
"The king and queen can choose," she says.

Bella sees some bunnies nearby.
They have long, silky ears and pink
noses. Bella gathers as many bunnies
as she can carry.

Georgia cannot pick just one pet, either!
She giggles as she puts six guinea pigs
in a wagon.

Next, they visit a nearby stream.
Molly holds out a large glass bowl.

Three glittery goldfish leap out of the water.
They land in Molly's bowl with a splash.

The last stop is a toadstool cottage.
A pack of puppies tumbles in the grass.
The puppies lick Lauren's legs.

She lifts the puppies into the wagon.

At last, they are on their
way to the Fairyland Palace.
One pony pulls the cart.
The other pulls the wagon.

The ponies are pulling a lot of pets!
"I wonder which pet the king and queen
will pick," Penny says.

All at once, a kitten jumps right into the
bunny crate.
A bunny bounds onto the brown pony's back.

The pony bolts forward, and the animals all charge through the palace gate.

The other pony jumps over a fountain, the wagon comes loose and the goldfish spill into the pool!

The king and queen huddle in the middle
of the palace garden.
The animals run, hop and gallop
around them.

"This isn't a parade," declares Katie.
"It's a stampede!"
"What should we do?" cries Bella.

"Maybe we need a magic spell," suggests
Lauren.

But then a sweet song rises above the squeaks, barks and whinnies.
Flit swoops around the animals.
The animals stop in their tracks.

Flit chirps a new song.
He flies in a straight line, and all the
animals follow.
The ponies, puppies and kittens march.

The bunnies hop.
The guinea pigs and hamsters scramble
along behind.
The goldfish do flips in the fountain.

The king and queen clap.
"Thank you, Pet Fairies," the king exclaims.
"What a grand pet parade."
"The animals are all lovely," the queen says,
"but the king and I cannot agree on one pet."
The Pet Fairies gasp.

"We would like them all to be our animal friends," the king explains.
"We promise to give them a safe, happy home," adds the queen.
The Pet Fairies think that sounds like a great decision.

"We'd also like to thank Flit," the queen says.
"He was a great help."
"Yes," says the king. "Flit will always be our special friend."
"Hooray for friends!" everyone cheers.
They can all agree on that!